Away
from
Home

Anita Lobel

Away from Home

Greenwillow Books New York

Watercolor and gouache paints were used for
the full-color art. The text type is Leawood.
Copyright © 1994 by Anita Lobel
All rights reserved. No part of this book may
be reproduced or utilized in any form or by
any means, electronic or mechanical, including
photocopying, recording, or by any information
storage and retrieval system, without permission
in writing from the Publisher, Greenwillow Books,
a division of William Morrow & Company, Inc.,
1350 Avenue of the Americas, New York, NY 10019.
Printed in Singapore by Tien Wah Press
First Edition 10 9 8 7 6 5 4 3 2 1

Library of Congress Cataloging-in-Publication Data

Lobel, Anita.
Away from home / by Anita Lobel.
    p.   cm.
Summary: Proceeds through the alphabet
using boys' names and the names of exotic
places in alliterative fashion.
ISBN 0-688-10354-5 (trade).
ISBN 0-688-10355-3 (lib. bdg.)
[1. Travel—Fiction.   2. Alphabet.]
I. Title.   PZ7.L7794Aw   1994   [E]—dc20
93-36521   CIP   AC

With love for Adam,
who likes nothing better than to be at home with his family

Adam arrived in Amsterdam.

Bernard ballooned in Barcelona.

Craig crawled in Cracow.

David danced in Detroit.

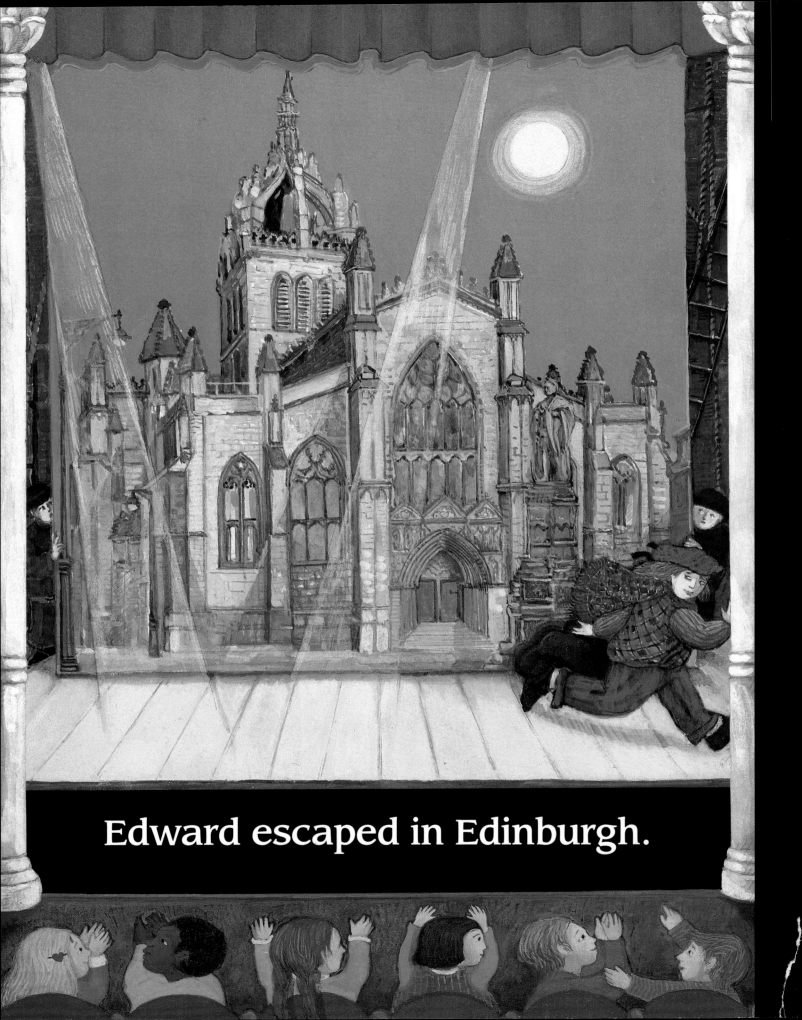

Edward escaped in Edinburgh.

Frederick fiddled in Florence.

Garrett gazed in Giza.

Henry hoped in Hollywood.

Isaac idled in Innsbruck.

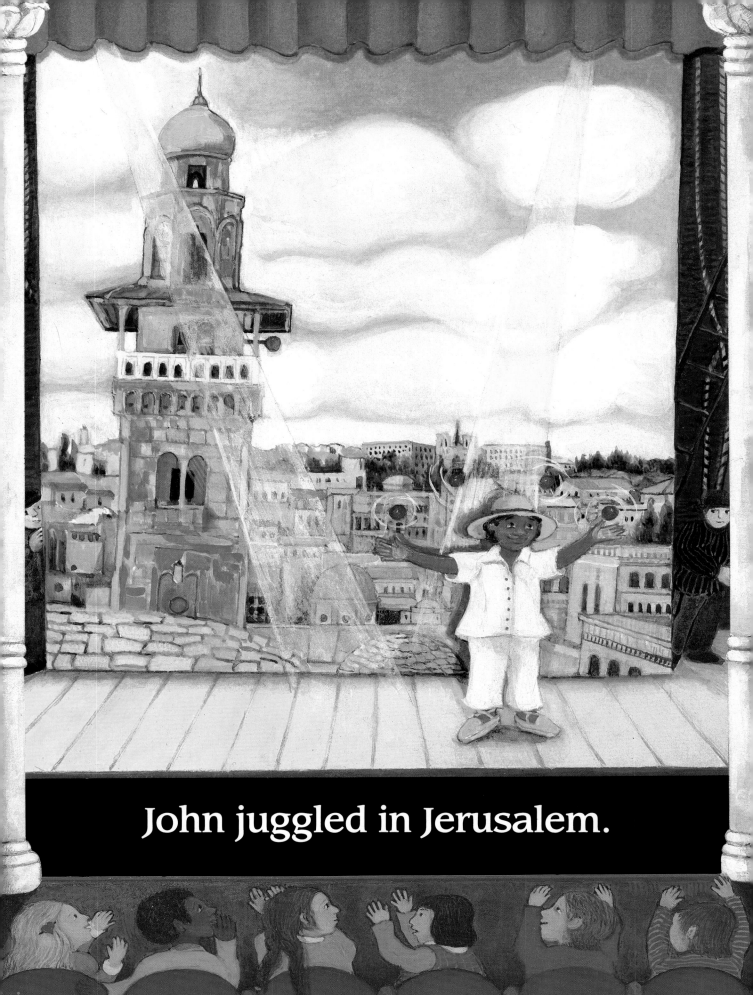

John juggled in Jerusalem.

Kevin knelt in Kyoto.

Lloyd limped in London.

Michael moped in Moscow.

Nathan nibbled in New York.

Oliver oscillated in Odense.

Paul painted in Paris.

Quincy quivered in Quebec.

Richard rolled in Rio.

Shaun sailed in Stockholm.

Thomas trumpeted in Tulsa.

Upton unpacked in Uxmal.

Vincent vacationed in Venice.

William waited in Washington.

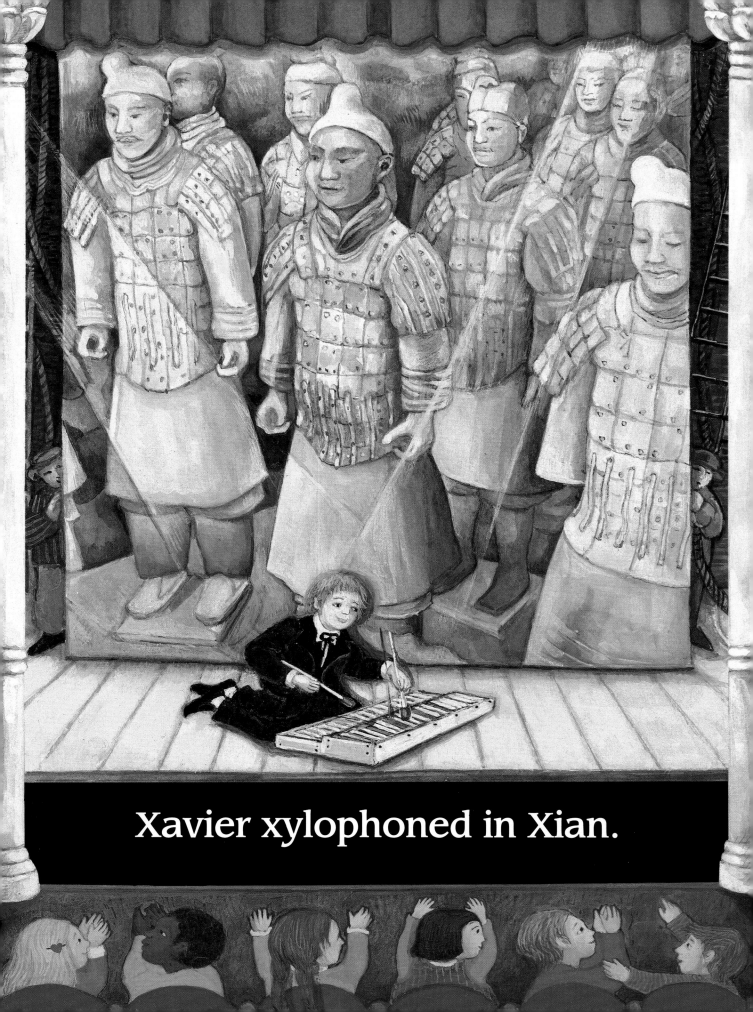

Xavier xylophoned in Xian.

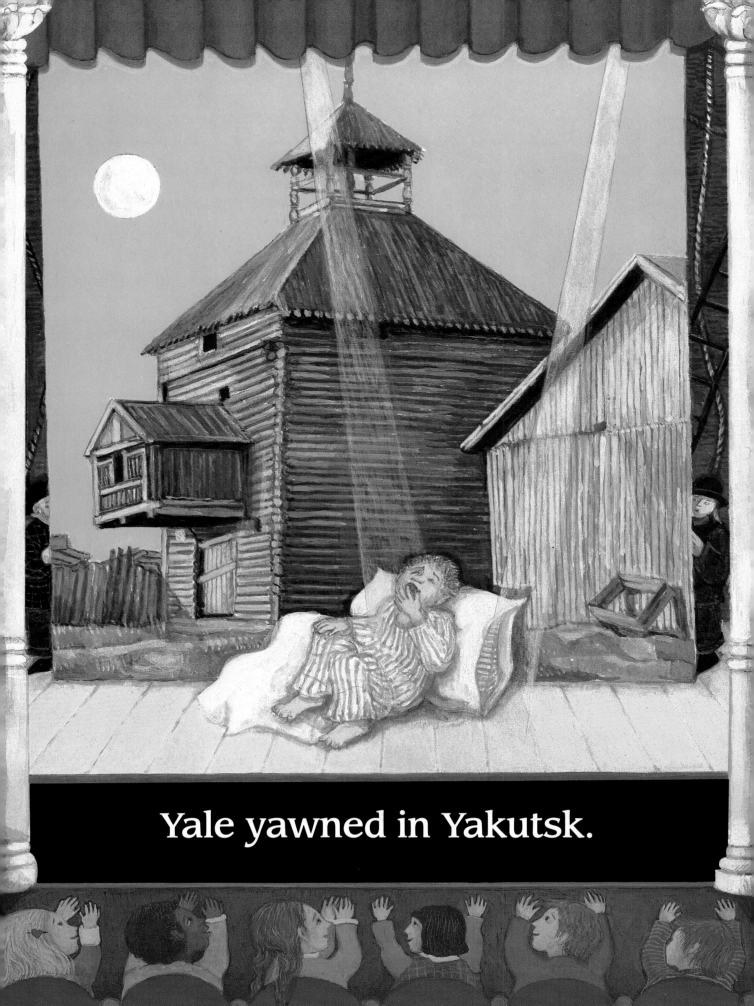

Yale yawned in Yakutsk.

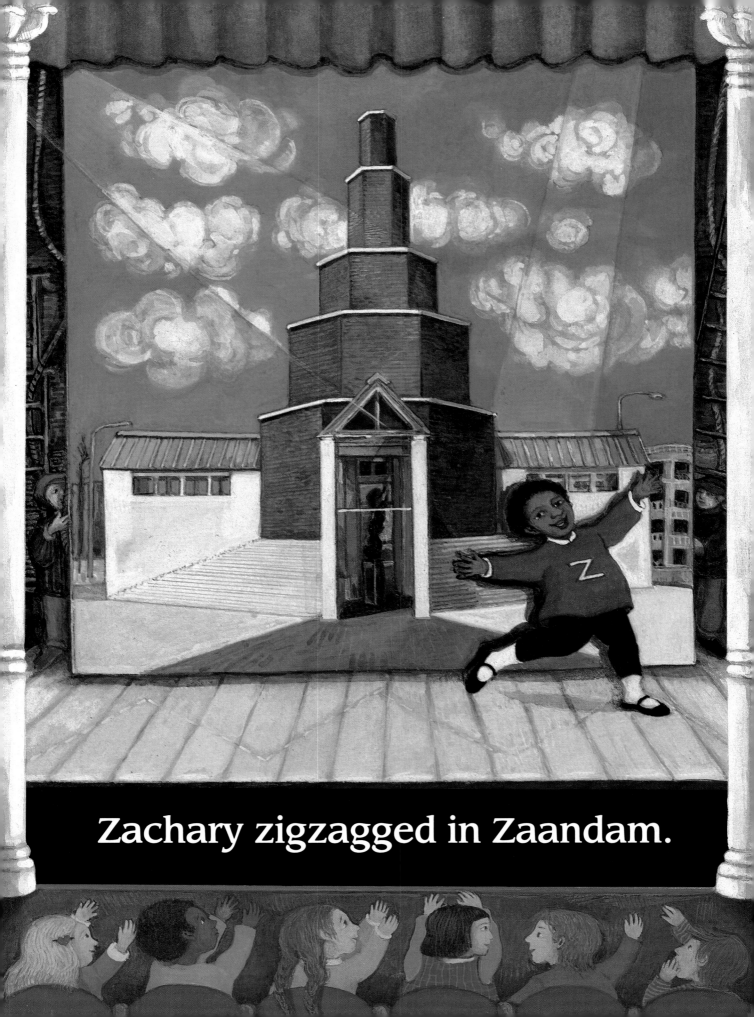

Zachary zigzagged in Zaandam.

WHERE THEY WENT

AMSTERDAM is a city in the Netherlands famous for its canals, art treasures, and houses that look like these.

BARCELONA is an elegant city in Spain. These towers crown the Templo de la Sagrada Familia, a cathedral designed by Antonio Gaudi.

CRACOW is the city in Poland where I was born. This is its central square.

DETROIT, Michigan, U.S.A., is the home of motor cars and Motown music. These are the buildings of its new Renaissance Center.

EDINBURGH is the capital of Scotland. This is the Cathedral of Saint Giles.

FLORENCE, Italy, is known for its art and architecture. This building, called the Baptistery, was built in the eleventh century.

GIZA is in Egypt. These ancient pyramids stand in the desert nearby.

HOLLYWOOD, California, U.S.A., is famous for its motion picture industry. Many actors come here hoping to be movie stars.

INNSBRUCK, Austria, has colorful houses along the Inn River. People from all over the world come to ski in the tall mountains nearby.

JERUSALEM is an ancient and holy city in Israel. This is the section known as the Old City.

KYOTO was once the capital of Japan. It has many temples and palaces like these.

LONDON is the capital of England. This is the Tower Bridge, which crosses the Thames River near the Tower of London.

MOSCOW is the capital of Russia. The great Cathedral of Saint Basil stands in Red Square.

NEW YORK, New York, U.S.A., is celebrated for many things, among them the Statue of Liberty and hot dogs from Nathan's Famous.

ODENSE, Denmark, is the birthplace of Hans Christian Andersen. This is the house in which he lived.

PARIS, the capital of France, has always been the home of celebrated authors and artists. This is the Cathedral of Notre Dame, one of the most famous churches in the world.

QUEBEC is the capital of the French-speaking Canadian province of the same name. This hotel, the Chateau Frontenac, stands on a hill above the St. Lawrence River.

RIO DE JANEIRO in Brazil is famous for this 120-foot-high statue of Christ the Redeemer, which looks down on the city from Corcovado Mountain.

STOCKHOLM, the capital of Sweden, is a city built on water. This is the City Hall.

TULSA, Oklahoma, where this statue of an oilman stands, is a center of the oil industry in the United States.

UXMAL, Mexico, is the site of this ruined temple that was built by the Mayas more than 1,000 years ago.

VENICE, Italy, is known for its canals, gondolas, art, and architecture. This church, the San Giorgio Maggiore, was designed by Palladio in the sixteenth century.

WASHINGTON, D.C., is the capital of the United States. This is the statue of Abraham Lincoln in the Lincoln Memorial.

XIAN is the city in China where more than 8,000 life-size soldiers made of clay were buried 2,000 years ago. They were not discovered until 1974.

YAKUTSK, Russia, lies in the cold, snowy region of Siberia. This log tower is part of an old fort.

ZAANDAM is a small city in the Netherlands. This modern building is an art gallery designed by Aldo Rossi.

HAPPY ABC JOURNEY TO ALL!

Anita Lobel 1994